ONE DATE TOO MANY

By Eleanor Robins

Development: Kent Publishing Services, Inc.
Design and Production: Signature Design Group, Inc.
Illustrations: Jan Naimo Jones

SADDLEBACK PUBLISHING, INC.
Three Watson
Irvine, CA 92618-2767

E-Mail: info@sdlback.com
Website: www.sdlback.com

ISBN 1-56254-689-9

Printed in the United States of America

1 2 3 4 5 6 0

One Date Too Many

Eleanor Robins
AR B.L.: 2.3
Points: 1.0   UG

Chapter 1

It was Monday. Paz was at lunch. Bel was with her.

Bel was her best friend. Bel's real name was Belinda.

The girls were talking about the spring dance.

Bel said, "Al called me last night."

Al was Bel's boyfriend. His real name was Alberto. He was on the baseball team. He and Bel had been dating for only a few weeks.

Bel said, "We talked about the dance. I can hardly wait. It is the first dance since Al and I started to date."

Paz was glad Bel had a date to the dance. She wished she did.

"I wish Cruz would ask me to the dance. But I don't think he will," Paz said.

Cruz was on the baseball team too. And he was very cute.

Bel said, "Maybe he will. He doesn't have a date."

"How do you know?" Paz asked.

"He was talking to Juan before math class started. And he told Juan he didn't have a date," Bel said.

Juan was on the track team. And he was in history class with Paz. But Cruz was not in a class with Paz.

"What else did you hear Cruz say?" Paz asked.

"That he does plan to go to the dance. But that is all I heard," Bel said.

"Do you really think Cruz might ask me?" Paz asked.

Bel thought about it. Then she said, "I don't know. But I do know one guy who wants to ask you."

"Who?" Paz asked.

"Juan," Bel said.

That surprised Paz.

"How do you know?" Paz asked.

"He asked me who you are going to the dance with," Bel said.

"What did you tell him?" Paz asked.

"That you didn't have a date," Bel said.

"Do you think he asked you for Cruz?" Paz asked.

She sure hoped he did.

Bel laughed.

Then she said, "No. I am sure he asked for himself. Because I think he likes you. And he wants to ask you to the dance."

"Did Cruz hear you talking to Juan?" Paz asked.

"I don't think so," Bel said.

Paz hoped he didn't.

Paz said, "Good. I like Juan OK. But I want to go to the dance with Cruz."

And she didn't want Cruz to think she might go with Juan.

Lunch time was almost over.

Bel said, "Cruz is coming this way. Maybe he wants to talk to you."

Paz sure hoped he did.

Bel said, "Juan is coming this way too. And he will get here first."

And Juan did get there first.

"Hi," he said to both girls.

"Hi," both girls said to him.

"I was looking for you. I am glad I saw you," Juan said. But he was looking only at Paz.

Oh, no. He was going to ask her to the dance. Paz was sure of it.

Just then Cruz walked by their table. But he did not stop.

A girl named Ana said something to Cruz. And he stopped to talk to her. Paz hoped he didn't ask her to the dance.

Then Paz thought about Juan. She had forgotten he had stopped to talk to her. She felt bad that she forgot.

Juan looked like he wanted to ask her something. But he just said, "Lunch time is over. I will talk to you later."

"OK," Paz said.

But she was thinking about Cruz. And not about what Juan said.

Juan walked away from the table.

Bel said, "I thought Juan was going to ask you to the dance."

Paz had thought so too. But she

wished Cruz would ask her. But she did not think he would.

Bel said, "We need to go. It will soon be time for class."

The girls quickly got up from the table. They put their trays up. Then they hurried out into the hall.

Cruz was in the hall just outside the lunchroom.

Why was he there?

Paz wished she could stop and talk to him. But she knew she could not do that.

So she just waved and walked by him.

Cruz said, "Paz. Wait up. I need to ask you something."

Paz stopped.

Was she wrong?

Was Cruz going to ask her to the dance?

Chapter 2

Bel said, "See you in class, Paz. Good luck."

Only Paz could hear what Bel said.

Bel hurried off. So Paz could talk to Cruz by herself.

Cruz walked up to Paz.

Cruz said, "What did you do in science today? We always do the same thing your class does."

"Lab work," Paz said.

Cruz said, "Good. Lab work is OK. One more thing. Do you—?"

But he didn't get to finish what he wanted to ask.

Griff came out of the lunch room.

Griff had English with Paz. And so did Bel. It was their next class. Coach Mann was their teacher.

Griff said, "You need to get to class, Paz. And you too, Cruz. So you won't be late."

Griff always got to class on time. But he did not always do his work.

Cruz said, "I need to go. Maybe I will ask you later."

What did he want to ask her? Was it about science? Or was he about to ask her to the dance?

Cruz walked off. And Paz hurried to class.

The bell rang as Paz walked into class. She quickly sat down in front of Bel.

"Did he ask you?" Bel asked.

"No," Paz said.

Paz wanted to tell Bel that Cruz

almost asked her something. But it was time for class to start.

Coach Mann called the roll. Then he said, "First we will go over your homework. So you can find out how you did on it."

The class went over the homework. Paz did OK. English was always hard for her. But she studied it a lot. So she had a good grade in the class.

Then Coach Mann said, "Now we will talk about your paper."

"What paper?" Griff asked.

"The one all of you have to write," Coach Mann said.

"Do we have to?" Griff asked.

Coach Mann said, "Yes, Griff. It needs to be five pages. And you have to turn it in next Friday."

"I don't want to write a five page paper," Griff said.

Coach Mann looked at Griff.

Then he said, "Then you can write a ten page paper, Griff. Would you like to do that? It is up to you."

Griff didn't say any more.

Coach Mann quit looking at Griff. And he looked back at the class.

He said, "What you write about is up to you."

Paz was glad to hear that.

Coach Mann talked some more about the paper. Then the bell rang.

Paz and Bel quickly got their books. And they hurried out into the hall.

Bel said, "What did Cruz want? I can hardly wait to find out."

Paz told her what Cruz said.

"Do you think he was going to ask you to the dance?" Bel asked.

Paz said, "Maybe. But it might have been about lab work."

But she sure hoped it wasn't.

Bel said, "I have to get to class. I wish we could talk some more after school. But I have to stay late. And rehearse for the play. And I have to come early tomorrow."

Bel was in a play. And she had to rehearse a lot for it.

Paz and Bel walked to and from school together. Now Paz would have to walk by herself. And she did not like to do that.

Chapter 3

Paz hoped she would see Cruz again before school was over. And she would find out what he wanted to ask her. But she did not see him.

Paz started to walk home. She wished she didn't have to walk by herself.

"Paz. Wait," Marge called to her.

Paz stopped to wait for Marge.

Marge was in her math class. And sometimes Marge ate lunch with Paz and Bel.

Marge hurried up to her.

Marge said, "I saw you talking to

Cruz after lunch. Did he ask you to the dance?"

Paz said, "No. He was asking me about science."

Marge looked like she didn't believe Paz. She said, "Why would he ask you about science?"

Paz said, "We have the same teacher. He wanted to know what my class did."

"Too bad. I guess you want to go with him. You do, don't you?" Marge said.

Paz did not answer.

"You do, don't you?" Marge asked again.

Paz did not want to lie to Marge. So she said, "Yes. I do."

Marge said, "I thought you did. Maybe he will call you tonight."

"I hope he will," Paz said.

But Paz did not think he would.

And Cruz didn't call her.

The next day Paz was on her way to lunch. She had not seen Cruz all morning. Maybe she would see him at lunch.

But Paz was not in a hurry to get to lunch. She would have to eat by herself. And she did not like to do that.

Bel was going to eat lunch with some girls in the play. So they could talk about the play.

Marge called to Paz. She said, "Paz. Wait."

Paz waited for Marge.

Marge hurried up to her.

"I didn't get to ask you after math. Did Cruz call you last night?" Marge said.

"No. He didn't," Paz said.

She wished Marge had not asked her.

Marge said, "You have to see Cruz as

soon as you can. And talk to him. So he can ask you to the dance."

The girls saw Cruz. He was almost to the lunch room.

Marge said, "Hurry, Paz. And maybe we can catch up to Cruz. Then you can tell him what you did in science. And maybe he will ask you to the dance."

Paz didn't want to catch up with Cruz. She thought he might guess what she was trying to do. But she had to keep up with Marge. So she hurried too.

The girls came up behind Cruz. He had just started to go in the lunchroom.

"Tell him," Marge said to Paz.

"I don't know," Paz said.

She did not like to talk to a boy first.

Marge gave Paz a push. And Paz bumped into Cruz.

Cruz stopped. And then he turned around. He looked surprised to see Paz.

Cruz didn't say anything. He just looked at her.

Paz had to say something. So she said, "Hi, Cruz. Do you want to know what we did in science?"

"Yeah. What?" Cruz asked.

Paz told him.

Griff came up behind them. He said, "Go on in, Cruz. I am ready to eat."

So Cruz did not stay and talk to Paz.

Marge said, "Oh, well. Too bad, Paz. Better luck next time. Let's go eat."

The girls quickly got their lunches and sat down.

Juan came over to their table. He looked at Paz.

"Is it OK for me to call you tonight?" he asked.

"Yes," Paz said.

Then Juan went to sit with some of his friends.

Why was Juan going to call her?

Paz hoped he wasn't going to ask her to the dance. She wanted Cruz to have some more time to ask her.

Marge said, "Why do you think Juan wants to call you? Do you think he is going to ask you to the dance?"

"I don't know," Paz said.

But she thought he might.

"Do you want to go with him? Or do you still want to go with Cruz?" Marge asked.

Paz did not want to answer. But she didn't want to be rude to Marge.

"I want to go with Cruz," Paz said.

"Then you should go with Cruz," Marge said.

But he had to ask Paz first. And Paz wasn't sure he would do that.

Chapter 4

Paz had to walk home by herself. Bel was at play rehearsal.

Paz did not see Marge. She didn't want to walk by herself. But she did not really want to walk with Marge.

Paz got home. And she started to work on her homework. She worked for a long time.

Paz stopped to help her mom cook dinner. Her family ate. And Paz helped her mom clean up the kitchen.

Then Paz worked on her homework some more.

The phone rang. Paz thought it was Juan. But it was Bel.

Bel said, "Hi, Paz. I just had to call. I have not had a chance to talk to you all day. Did Juan ask you to the dance? Or did Cruz?"

Paz said, "No. But at lunch Juan asked to call me tonight."

Bel said, "That is very good, Paz. I think he will ask you to the dance. I know he wants to."

"I am not sure I want him to ask me," Paz said.

Bel said, "Oh, Paz. You still want Cruz to ask you. But you should not plan on that. Juan might ask you. Go with him. I think you would have a good time."

But he would not be Cruz.

Paz wished she knew who Cruz was going to ask.

Bel said, "I can't eat with you tomorrow. I must eat with the girls in the play.

So we can talk about the play. But I don't have rehearsal. So I can walk to school with you. And walk home with you."

Paz was glad to hear that.

Bel said, "I have to go now. Al is going to call me."

"OK," Paz said.

Paz went back to her homework. But it was hard to keep her mind on it. She was thinking about the dance.

The phone rang again.

Paz hoped it was Cruz. But she thought it was Juan. And it was.

Paz hoped he didn't call to ask her to the dance.

Juan said, "Hi, Paz. This is Juan. Did you get all of the notes in history today?"

"Yes," Paz said.

Paz felt better. Maybe he called just to ask her about school work.

Paz told Juan what he wanted to know about the notes.

Juan said, "Thanks for your help."

Juan didn't say anything right away.

But then Juan said, "Do you—?"

Then Juan stopped talking.

Paz said, "What?"

But she was not sure she wanted to know.

At first Juan did not say any more. Then he said, "I will see you in history tomorrow."

"OK," Paz said.

Had Juan called just to ask about history?

Or had he planned to ask her to the dance?

Chapter 5

The next day Paz was at lunch. She was looking for a table.

Marge was sitting at a table. She waved to Paz.

"Paz. Over here," she yelled to Paz.

Paz didn't want to eat with Marge. But she did not want to eat by herself. And she did not want to be rude to Marge.

Paz went over to Marge's table and sat down.

Marge said, "Great news, Paz. I can hardly wait to tell you."

"What?" Paz asked.

Marge said, "I heard Cruz talking to

Griff. Cruz is going to call a girl right after school. And ask her to the dance."

"Who?" Paz asked.

Marge said, "I didn't hear her name. But they had been talking about you. So I am sure it is you. So stay by your phone."

Did Paz dare hope Cruz would call her? Or was it too good to be true?

"Call me just as soon as you can after Cruz calls you. And tell me what he said," Marge said.

"OK," Paz said. But she didn't really want to call Marge.

Paz could hardly wait to get to English class. And tell Bel what Marge said.

Paz got to class as soon as she could. But Bel was almost late.

Paz said, "I have some news to tell you, Bel. And it is very good."

But the bell rang. And Paz didn't get to say more to Bel.

Paz had to hurry to her next class. So she did not get to talk to Bel after English class.

Paz could hardly wait for school to be over. She knew none of the teams had practice after school. So Cruz could call her as soon as she got home.

Paz was happy to hear the end of school bell ring.

Paz met Bel. And the two girls started to walk home.

Bel said, "You have a big smile on your face, Paz. Why are you so happy? And what is your news?"

"Marge heard Cruz talking to Griff. She is sure Cruz is going to call me. And ask me to the dance," Paz said.

"Don't get your hopes up, Paz. A lot of times Marge gets things mixed up.

She may have this time too," Bel said.

But Paz was sure Marge must be right.

Paz was glad when she got home. So she would be there for her call from Cruz.

Paz tried to do her homework. But she could not keep her mind on her work.

The phone rang.

Paz hurried to the phone. She hoped it was Cruz.

But it was Marge. Not Cruz.

Why was she calling?

"I have some bad news for you," Marge said.

"What?" Paz asked.

Marge said, "I just found this out. So I called you just as soon as I did."

"What?" Paz asked again.

But she was not sure she wanted to know.

"Cruz called Ana to ask her to the dance. But she wasn't at home. He is going to call her later. I am sure she will go with him," Marge said.

Paz was sure she would too.

Marge said, "Too bad, Paz. I was sure he was going to ask you."

Paz thanked Marge for calling her.

It was too good to be true that Cruz might ask her. She should have known that all along.

Chapter 6

Paz called Bel. She wanted to tell Bel about Cruz.

"Did Cruz call you?" Bel asked.

Paz said, "No. Marge did. Marge said Cruz called Ana. She was not home. But he is going to call her later. So he will take her to the dance."

"I am sorry, Paz," Bel said.

Paz did not feel like talking about Cruz any longer.

"I have to stop talking. I must do my homework," Paz said.

Bel said, "OK. We can talk more at lunch tomorrow."

Paz tried to get busy on her

homework. But she could not keep her mind on it.

She had really wanted Cruz to ask her to the dance.

Paz worked a little at a time on her homework. It took her a long time to finish.

The phone rang. Paz hurried to the phone.

Could it be Cruz after all?

But it was Juan. Not Cruz.

Why did he call?

Juan said, "Hi, Paz. This is Juan. Are you doing your homework?"

"No. I have done it all," Paz said.

"I have too," Juan said.

So he was not calling about homework.

Juan didn't say any more right away. But then he said, "Do you have a date to the dance?"

"No," Paz said.

What else could she say? She didn't have a date.

"Do you want to go with me?" Juan asked.

"Yes," Paz said.

What else could she say? He knew she did not have a date. And she didn't want to make him feel bad.

And she did want to go to the dance. And she knew now that Cruz was not going to ask her.

Juan said, "Then it is a date, Paz. I will talk to you later."

Paz liked Juan. But she liked Cruz more.

She still wanted to go to the dance with Cruz.

But what did it matter? Cruz was

going to the dance with Ana.

Paz called Bel. Paz wanted to tell Bel that Juan called. And she had a date to go to the dance with him. But Bel was not home.

Paz did not call Marge.

But Marge called Paz a few minutes later.

Marge said, "Great news, Paz. Cruz isn't going to the dance with Ana."

"How do you know?" Paz asked.

Marge said, "Cruz called her again. And she has a date. So maybe he will ask you now."

"It is too late," Paz said.

"Why?" Marge asked.

"Juan asked me to the dance. And I said I would go with him," Paz said.

"I didn't think you wanted to go with Juan. I thought you wanted to go with Cruz," Marge said.

Paz said, "I do. But I like Juan OK. And you told me Cruz was going to ask Ana."

Marge said, "And I am glad I told you that. You needed to know Cruz was going to ask her."

Paz was not sure she did need to know that. And she wished Marge had not told her.

Maybe then she would not have told Juan she would go with him.

Chapter 7

Paz wanted very much to talk to Bel. But Bel had to go to school early the next day. So Paz didn't see her before school.

Paz hoped she would see Bel in the hall before lunch. But she didn't.

Lunch time came. Paz hurried to lunch.

Bel was waiting for Paz at the lunch room door.

Bel said, "I have some very good news for you, Paz. Al just told me."

"What?" Paz asked.

She needed to hear some very good news.

Bel said, "Let's get our lunch first. And I will tell you after we sit down."

"OK," Paz said.

What could the very good news be?

Paz and Bel got their lunches. Then they looked for a table.

Marge waved at them. She was sitting at a table.

She said, "Paz. Bel. Over here. You can sit with me."

Bel said, "I don't want to sit with Marge. But I don't want us to be rude to her. So we should sit with her."

"OK," Paz said.

The girls went to Marge's table and sat down.

Paz didn't want to ask Bel about the very good news with Marge there. But Paz wanted to know what it was.

"What is your very good news?" she asked.

At first Bel did not answer. But then she said, "I don't have to tell you now. I can tell you later."

"Tell her now. I want to hear it too," Marge said.

Bel looked like she didn't want to say what it was. But she did.

Bel said, "Al just told me this. So it is true. Cruz did call Ana. But she has a date. So Cruz is not going to the dance with her."

Marge said, "Is that your news? Paz and I already knew that."

"No. There is more," Bel said.

What could it be?

"Cruz asked Al who you were going to the dance with. Al told him you didn't have a date. So Cruz is going to call you tonight. And ask you to go with him," Bel said.

But it was too late now for Paz to go with him.

"What is wrong, Paz? You don't look well," Bel said.

Marge said, "Do you want me to tell her, Paz? Or do you want to tell her?"

"I will tell Bel," Paz said.

Paz looked at Bel.

Then Paz said, "It is too late, Bel. I have a date."

"You do?" Bel said. She looked very surprised.

"Yes. With Juan," Marge said.

Paz wished Marge had let her tell Bel.

"When did Juan ask you?" Bel asked.

Paz said, "He called after I talked to you. I called you again. To tell you. But you were not home."

Bel said, "That is very good news, Paz. I am glad Juan asked you. Now you know for sure you have a date to the dance. You don't have to hope Cruz will really call you."

Marge said, "I don't think it's good news. Paz wants to go with Cruz. Not Juan."

"But Paz has already said she will go with Juan," Bel said.

"What are you going to tell Cruz when he calls?" Marge asked.

"That I have a date with Juan," Paz said.

She did not want to tell him that. But she would have to tell him that.

"Why?" Marge asked.

"Because I do," Paz said.

"Cruz doesn't know that. Tell him you will go with him. And tell Juan something came up. And you can't go with him," Marge said.

Bel didn't say anything. But Paz was sure Bel did not think Marge was right.

Paz said, "I can't do that. Juan would see me at the dance with Cruz. And that would make Juan feel bad."

"So? He will get over it," Marge said.

"I do not want to hurt Juan. He is a nice guy," Paz said.

"Don't worry about Juan. Do what you want to do," Marge said.

"I don't think I can do that," Paz said.

Paz would not want a guy to treat her that way. But she knew some girls did that. So they could date the guy they liked better.

Marge said, "Why? You like Cruz better. So go with the guy you like better. You have to say you will go. Or he might not ask you out again."

Marge was right about that. He might not. Some guys didn't like to get turned down for a date. So they didn't ask the girl out again.

And she wanted Cruz to ask her out more than one time.

But she already had a date.

What should she do?

Chapter 8

Paz met Bel after school. Bel did not have play rehearsal. So Paz could walk home with her.

Paz was glad they didn't see Marge. Paz wanted to talk to Bel with no one else around.

The girls started to walk home.

Bel said, "I saw Juan after lunch. He told me he was going to the dance with you. He is so happy you are going with him. But he is worried you might break the date."

"Does he know Cruz might ask me?" Paz asked.

Bel said, "I don't think he does. I

think he is worried because he likes you so much."

Paz knew Juan must like her. Since he asked her to the dance. But she did not know he liked her a lot.

"I hope you aren't thinking about breaking your date with him," Bel said.

Paz did not say anything.

Bel stopped walking. She looked at Paz.

Bel said, "Tell me, Paz. Are you thinking about breaking your date with Juan?"

Paz said slowly, "I don't know. Juan is a nice guy. But I would like to go with Cruz."

"You gave Juan your word, Paz," Bel said.

Paz said, "I know. But Marge is right. Cruz might not ask me out again."

"Don't be like Marge. That is all I can say. It is your choice. Do what you must do," Bel said.

Bel was right. It was her choice. But that did not make Paz feel better.

"I don't know what to do," Paz said.

"Then think about it for a while. You do not have to make up your mind now. Cruz will not call until tonight," Bel said.

Paz studied some when she got home. But it was hard to keep her mind on her work.

Then she helped cook dinner.

Paz kept thinking about what she should do. She thought and thought about what Marge said. Maybe Marge was right. Why not do what she wanted to do? And go with the guy she liked better?

Her family ate dinner. Then Paz helped to clean up the kitchen.

Paz started to do her school work again. But she kept waiting for the phone to ring.

The phone rang. Paz hurried to the phone.

Was it Cruz?

But it was not Cruz. It was Juan.

Had Juan found out that Cruz might call her? Was he calling to break the date?

But Paz didn't think he was.

So why was he calling?

Juan said, "Hi, Paz. This is Juan. I do not have to know now. But what color dress will you wear to the dance?"

"I don't know yet," Paz said.

"Please tell me when you do. I want to get you some flowers," Juan said.

That surprised Paz. She said, "That would be nice, Juan. I will let you know the color."

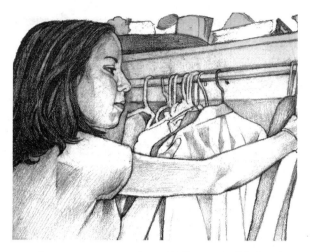

Juan was so nice. Why couldn't she be happy about going to the dance with him?

Why did she still want to go with Cruz?

It was not long until the phone rang again.

Was it Cruz?

Paz hurried to the phone.

It was Cruz.

What should she do?

"Want to go to the dance with me?" Cruz asked.

Paz wanted so much to go to the dance with Cruz.

But no one made her say she would go with Juan. It was her choice.

Paz wished she could go with both Cruz and Juan. But she could not do that. That would be one date too many.

Paz gave her word to Juan. And she would keep it.

"Thank you for asking me, Cruz. But I can't go with you. I already have a date with Juan," Paz said.

"So? Tell him you have made new plans. Plans to go with me," Cruz said. Then he laughed.

But Paz would not tell Juan that. Paz would go with Juan. And she would have a good time. Maybe a better time than she would have had with Cruz.